Springs and Things

Written by Catherine Baker
Illustrated by Neil Sutherland, Blue-Zoo and Tony Trimmer

S was feeling sad.
"Tut! Tut!" said T. "This will
not do! Join in with us!"

ch-**e**-**s**-**t**, chest!
It was a big chest ...
and it was shut.

3

S was feeling better now.
"We have got to see what is in
the chest!" she said.

S undid the string on the chest.
"I cannot shift the lid," she said.

"We can help!" said **T**.

s-**t**-**r**-**o**-**ng**, strong!

"Smashing!" said S. "Look at
my strong arms!"

Now I can lift the lid!

There was a spring with
a little chair on the end!

S got into the chair and did up the strap. The chair shot up into the air!

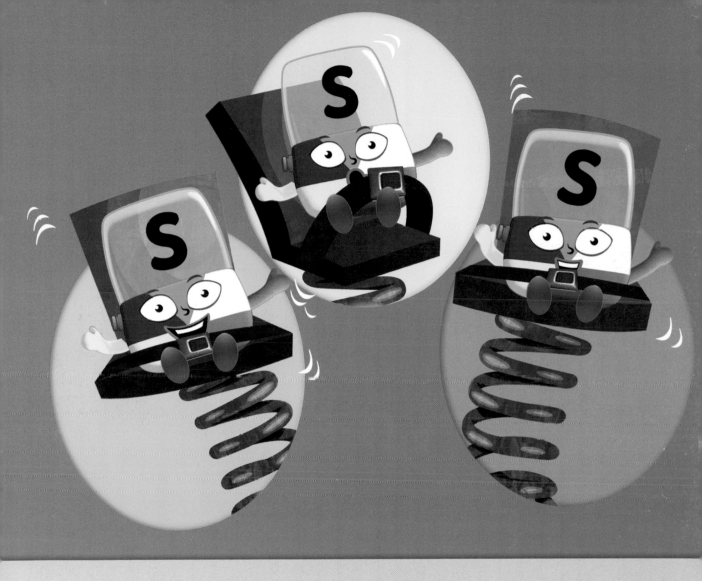

S was zooming up and
down like a jack-in-the-box!

"It looks like fun in that chair,"
said CH, "but there is no
room for us!"

But s had a splendid plan.
"We need some extra chests!"
she said.

ch-e-**s**-t-**s**, chests!
All of a sudden, there were three chests!

CH undid the string on one of the chests.

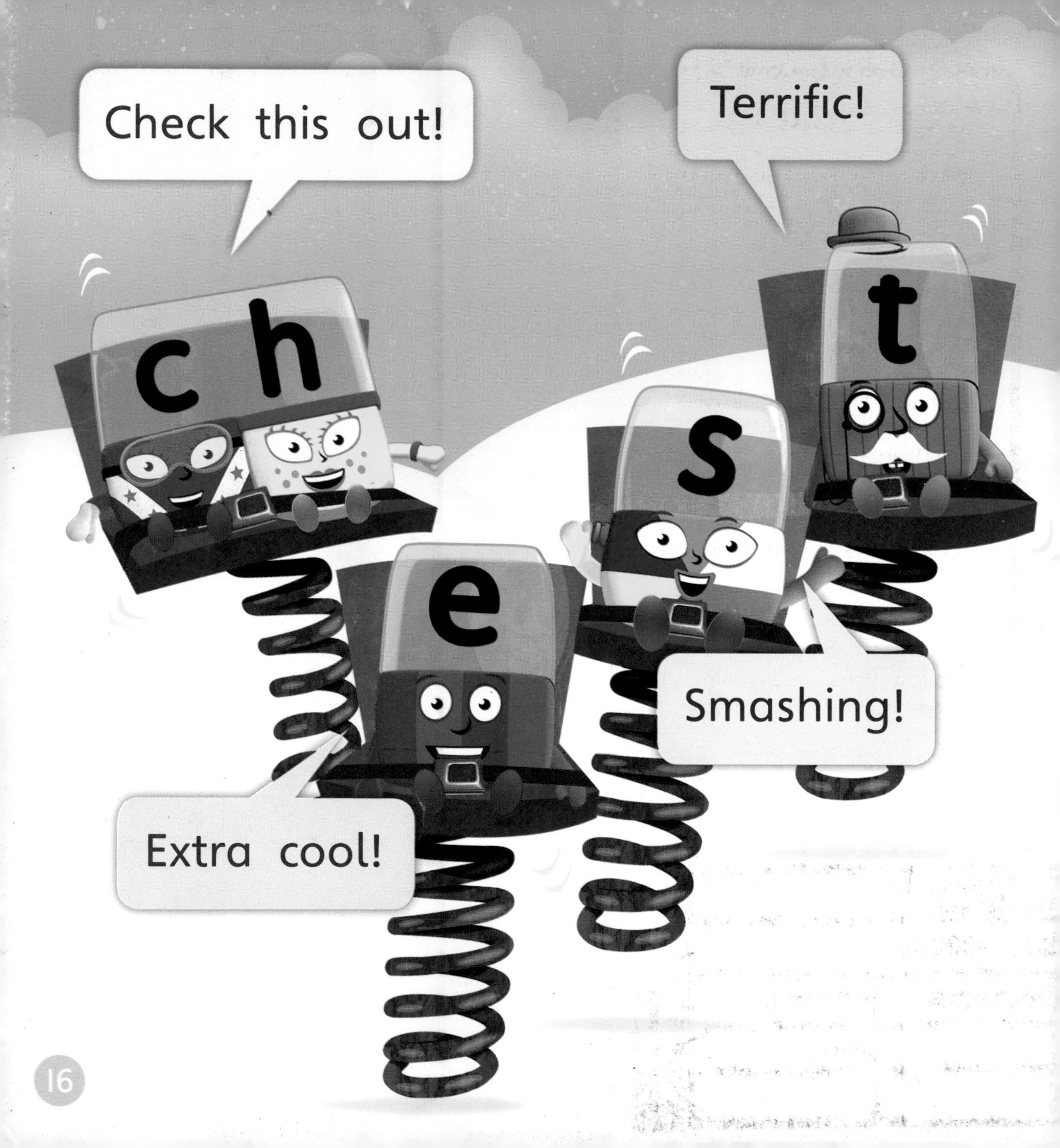
Check this out!
Terrific!
c h
s
t
e
Smashing!
Extra cool!